YOU
BE
THE
JURY

Courtroom V

Also by MARVIN MILLER

YOU BE THE JURY

Courtroom V

Marvin Miller

Interior illustrations by Colin Mier

SCHOLASTIC INC.
New York Toronto London Auckland Sydney

ISBN 0-590-73910-7

Text copyright © 1995 by Marvin Miller. Illustrations copyright © 1995 by Colin Mier. All rights reserved. Published by Scholastic Inc., 555 Broadway, New York, NY 10012, by arrangement with Scholastic Publications Ltd.

12 11 10 9 8 7 6 5 4   7 8 9/9 0 1/0

Printed in the U.S.A.   40

First Scholastic printing, April 1996

...for Robby, again ...

THE CASE OF THE
CARELESS SHOPPER

11

THE CASE OF THE
TRICKED MAGICIAN

22

THE CASE OF THE
FLOATING LOGS

35

THE CASE OF THE
SLOPPY EATER

46

**THE CASE OF THE
MISSING HOUSEKEEPER**

56

**THE CASE OF THE
STOLEN ANTIQUE**

67

**THE CASE OF THE
BARGAIN BEDROOM SUITE**

78

**THE CASE OF THE
TORN SHIRT**

91

**THE CASE OF THE
REFRIGERATOR BREAKDOWN**

102

**THE CASE OF THE
RUNAWAY CAR**

113

ORDER IN THE COURT

LADIES AND GENTLEMEN OF THE JURY:

This court is now in session. My name is Judge John Dennenberg. You are the jury, and the trials are set to begin.

You have a serious responsibility. Will the innocent be sent to jail and the guilty go free? Let's hope not. Your job is to make sure that justice is served.

Read each case carefully. Study the evidence presented and then decide.

GUILTY OR NOT GUILTY??

Both sides of the case will be presented to you. The person who has the complaint is called the *plaintiff*. He or she has brought the case to court.

The person being accused is called the *defendant*. The defendant is pleading his or her innocence and presents a much different version of what happened.

IN EACH CASE, THREE PIECES OF EVIDENCE WILL BE PRESENTED AS EXHIBITS A, B AND C. EXAMINE THE EXHIBITS VERY CAREFULLY. A *CLUE* TO THE SOLUTION OF EACH CASE WILL BE FOUND THERE. IT WILL DIRECTLY POINT TO THE INNOCENCE OR GUILT OF THE ACCUSED.

Remember, each side will try to convince you that his or her version is what actually happened. BUT YOU MUST MAKE THE FINAL DECISION.

THE CASE OF THE
CARELESS SHOPPER

LADIES AND GENTLEMEN OF THE JURY:

A supermarket must take reasonable care to make sure that it is a safe place to shop. If a customer is accidentally injured, the shop may be guilty of negligence.

Shirley Wexler, the plaintiff, accuses Extra-Fine Supermarket of failing to clean up a broken jar of olives that was dropped by another shopper. She slid on the oil and fell. The supermarket claims that Mrs Wexler, herself, caused the accident.

The plaintiff testified as follows:

"My name is Shirley Wexler. I live on Fairview Lane, about two blocks from Extra-Fine Supermarket.

"I invited some friends from work over to my house for a Saturday night dinner party. I did all my shopping on Friday.

"I spent the whole of Saturday afternoon preparing the dinner. My boss was going to be there, so everything had to be just perfect. I was so nervous, I ruined the apple pie I was baking. I even cut myself peeling a cucumber.

"I was mixing a salad when I realized it needed more olives. My boss just loves the green juicy ones. I had bought one jar the day before, but I thought the salad needed more. So I ran over to Extra-Fine Supermarket to buy another jar.

"As I walked over to the shelf where the olives were, I began to slide and fell flat on my back with a thud. My head hit the floor."

After Shirley Wexler fell down, a shop assistant helped her to her feet. As she stood up, she looked down at the floor. A broken jar of plump olives lay there, the slippery juice forming a big puddle. Another shopper must have broken it.

The supermarket manager, John Trilling, arrived and helped Mrs Wexler into his office. He asked her to sit down to recover from the shock of her fall.

EXHIBIT A is a photo of Mrs Wexler inside the manager's office.

Mrs Wexler continued her testimony:

"Mr Trilling was very kind. He seemed

concerned and asked how I felt. I was a little dizzy, but after a while I began to feel better, so I thanked him and went back to buy the olives."

While Mrs Wexler was entertaining her guests that evening, she suddenly felt a sharp throbbing pain across her forehead. The headache lasted all evening. She could barely join in the dinner conversation.

The next day the pain became worse. Shirley Wexler visited her doctor. He gave her a prescription for the headache.

But the medicine didn't help. Mrs Wexler's pain became unbearable. It only stopped hurting when she lay down.

Mrs Wexler's headaches lasted for three weeks. She had to lie down for hours at a time and was unable to go to work.

Mrs Wexler is suing Extra-Fine Supermarket for negligence because they failed to clean up the slippery olive spill. She wants the shop to compensate her for loss of earnings while she was out of work.

John Trilling, the supermarket manager, took the stand and claimed that his shop was not responsible for Mrs Wexler's injury. He testified as follows:

"We often have shoppers who knock over merchandise when they reach for an item on a shelf. Sometimes they break things without reporting it. They hope no one will find out.

"Our staff are very careful about accidents. They patrol the aisles continually. When they see a breakage, they are instructed to clean it up immediately."

Mr Trilling claims that the accident happened because Mrs Wexler dropped the olive jar and broke it herself.

"Everyone in our shop knows Mrs Wexler. She's always in a hurry. She dashes into our shop as though she's running a race and zips up and down the aisles.

"I once saw Mrs Wexler knock down a whole display. We all talk about her shopping habits. She always reaches for items on the back row of shelves, and leaves the shelves looking untidy."

Mr Trilling offered further proof to support his claim that Mrs Wexler was the person who dropped the jar of olives that she slipped on. He entered as evidence EXHIBIT B. It is a photograph taken after Mrs Wexler was helped into his office, and it shows the slippery puddle that caused her fall.

"Can you see the big pieces of broken glass and the olives and juice? It would have been impossible for someone to walk over to the shelf without noticing it first.

"If the olive jar had been broken by another shopper, Mrs Wexler certainly would have seen the mess. But if she had dropped the jar herself, she could easily have slipped on the puddle as she walked away."

The supermarket manager saved the pieces of glass from the broken olive jar. He thought they might be needed.

When Mrs Wexler sued his store for negligence, the manager had the glass pieces examined for fingerprints.

EXHIBIT C is a photograph of the fingerprints taken from the broken glass. There are several prints on the glass, including a clear set of Mrs Wexler's. The defence says this is proof that Wexler is the one who held the jar and then dropped it.

Mrs Wexler admits that the fingerprints are hers. But she can explain how they got on to the glass. She says that when she bought the first jar of olives on Friday, the day before the accident, she picked up one jar and then replaced it on the shelf and chose another.

Mrs Wexler insists that on Saturday another shopper broke the olive jar she had handled. Extra-Fine Supermarket is responsible for not cleaning up the mess.

LADIES AND GENTLEMEN OF THE JURY:

You have just heard the Case of the Careless Shopper. You must decide the merits of Shirley Wexler's claim. Be sure to examine carefully the evidence in EXHIBITS A, B and C.

Did Shirley Wexler slip on the puddle of olive juice after another shopper broke the jar? Or was she responsible for the breakage herself?

EXHIBIT A

EXHIBIT B

EXHIBIT C

FINGERPRINT REPORT

SOURCE _glass from broken olive jar_
Extra-fine Supermarket

DATE _March 26, 1995_

RIGHT HAND

1 THUMB	2 INDEX FINGER	3 MIDDLE FINGER	4 RING FINGER	5 LITTLE FINGER

COMPARISON

The above fingerprints match prints
of Shirley Wexler.
This analysis proves positive
identification because each
print exactly matches those of
the subject.
NOTE. Other prints were also
found on the broken glass.

VERDICT

ANOTHER SHOPPER BROKE THE OLIVE JAR.

Mrs Wexler said that she cut herself when she was preparing dinner on Saturday afternoon, before she went to the supermarket. In EXHIBIT A, she is shown in the manager's office after she slipped on the puddle. A bandage is wrapped around her right thumb.

In EXHIBIT C, her fingerprints from the broken olive jar show a clear impression of Mrs Wexler's right thumb. There is no sign of a bandage.

Therefore, Mrs Wexler handled the jar of olives on Friday, before she cut her thumb. That is how her prints got on to it. The following day, another customer picked up the jar and then dropped it.

21

THE CASE OF THE
TRICKED MAGICIAN

LADIES AND GENTLEMEN OF THE JURY:

A contract is a legal promise between two people. It can be enforced by a court of law. If one person breaks a written contract, the other can take legal action.

The case you will hear today is very unusual. Magnus Marvelo, the plaintiff, is a professional magician. He is suing Nancy Winslow for revealing the secret of his most famous magic trick. Miss Winslow admits that she exposed the trick, but insists that there was no reason why she could not do so.

Magnus Marvelo testified as follows:

"Ladies and gentlemen and children of all ages, I am The Great Marvelo! Oh, excuse me. That's how I begin my stage performance. I shall start again.

"Ahem! Ladies and gentlemen, my name is

Magnus Marvelo. I have been a professional magician for eighteen years. I have performed in the greatest theatres the world over.

"My star trick is a closely guarded secret. Completely surrounded by the audience, I saw a woman in half. Then I join her back together. No one has ever worked out how I do this.

"I was engaged to perform at the Lyric Theatre for the week beginning 20th November. But the day before my show opened, my lovely assistant Wanda developed appendicitis. She had to go to hospital for four days and then rest in bed."

Marvelo was frantic. Wanda was the only other person who had ever worked on the trick with him. She was the woman he sawed in half. Someone would have to take her place. He rushed to the theatre office to see if he could find a substitute. That is where he met Nancy Winslow, whose father owned the Lyric Theatre.

"I asked Miss Winslow if she would take Wanda's place and I would teach her how to perform the illusion. I offered to pay her $200 for the week. She agreed immediately.

"During our rehearsal, I became worried that Nancy might expose my trick afterwards. I asked her to sign a secrecy agreement that promised she would not reveal how the trick was done.

"I asked the stage manager for a sheet of paper and wrote out a statement which I asked Nancy to sign. I told her it was the same as a contract, and in it she agreed not to reveal how my sawing-in-half trick was done. Nancy read the paper and signed it."

But the day after The Great Marvelo's final performance, an usher showed him a copy of the local newspaper. There, on the front page, was an interview with Nancy Winslow, in which she revealed the secret of Marvelo's trick.

This newspaper article appears as EXHIBIT A. It shows exactly how Marvelo sawed Nancy in half. She secretly sank down into the middle of the platform that supported the box.

"When I read the newspaper, I couldn't believe my eyes!" said Marvelo. "My act was ruined! A magician's success depends on keeping the method of his trick a secret."

The Great Marvelo is suing Nancy Winslow for damaging his reputation and for the cost of developing a baffling new illusion. Marvelo claims that Nancy broke the written contract.

A lawyer for the magician has entered into evidence EXHIBIT B. It is the secrecy agreement signed by Miss Winslow.

The plaintiff's lawyer called Troy Lightfoot to the stand. Mr Lightfoot is the stage manager at the Lyric Theatre. Marvelo claims that Lightfoot saw Nancy Winslow sign the agreement.

Mr Lightfoot testified as follows:

"It was the day before Marvelo's performance. I was working on the stage, setting up the lighting. Marvelo and Nancy had just finished practising the sawing-in-half trick. They were talking to each other.

"Then Marvelo called out to me and asked if I had a blank sheet of paper. He said that he wanted Nancy to sign something.

"I had a notepad in the tool box that I kept behind the back curtain. I went back stage, tore out a blank sheet, and brought it out to Marvelo.

"As I was walking away, I saw Marvelo writing on the paper. Then he handed it to Nancy and asked her to sign it."

Nancy Winslow explained to the court that she had done nothing unlawful. She testified as follows:

Q: Do you admit that you told a newspaper reporter how Marvelo's sawing-in-half trick worked?

A: Of course I did. The reporter described the secret exactly the way I explained it to him.

Q: Marvelo claims that you signed an agreement that promised not to expose his famous trick. Is that your signature on the paper?

A: That looks like my signature, but it's not. I never signed that paper. Marvelo must have forged my name.

Miss Winslow explained that Marvelo had insisted she arrive at least an hour before every performance so that they could rehearse the trick until it was perfect. He made her agree that if she did not show up early each evening, he could cancel the performance and still be paid by her father.

"I couldn't understand why Marvelo was so worried," Nancy Winslow continued. "I told him I was reliable. But he said he wanted me to agree to this in writing.

"I remember that he asked Troy Lightfoot for some paper. Marvelo wrote down that I would agree to arrive one hour early each evening to practise. I read the paper and then I signed it. That is what was written on the paper that Lightfoot saw me sign. It was not a secrecy agreement."

Miss Winslow believes that after The Great Marvelo saw his trick exposed in the newspaper, he took another sheet of paper from the notebook in Troy Lightfoot's tool box. Then he wrote out a fake secrecy agreement and forged her signature at the bottom. He could easily have copied her handwriting from the first paper that she had signed.

A handwriting expert examined the secrecy contract. His opinion appears in EXHIBIT C. Although the expert states that the handwriting is remarkably similar to Nancy Winslow's signature, he cannot definitely conclude that it was signed by her.

Therefore, there is no absolute proof that Nancy Winslow actually signed the secrecy agreement.

Miss Winslow claims there was no written secrecy contract between herself and The Great Marvelo. She was not legally bound from revealing how the trick was done. Miss Winslow asks the court to dismiss the charges against her.

LADIES AND GENTLEMEN OF THE JURY:
You have just heard the Case of the Tricked Magician. You must decide the merits of The

Great Marvelo's claim. Be sure to examine carefully the evidence in EXHIBITS A, B and C.

Did Nancy Winslow sign the written contract promising to keep The Great Marvelo's sawing-in-half trick secret? Or was the agreement a forgery by Marvelo?

EXHIBIT A

MAGICIAN APPEARS AT THE LYRIC THEATRE

Master magician, The Great Marvelo, has completed a week of sold-out performances at the Lyric Theatre.

The highlight of Marvelo's performance was the sawing-in-half of local resident Nancy Winslow. In an exclusive interview with this newspaper, Nancy explains how the trick is performed.

Marvelo saws Nancy in half, and then joins her back together.

THE SECRET

Nancy enters the box, the ends of which allow her head, hands and feet to protrude. Nancy secretly sinks down into the middle of the platform which supports the box.

When the box has been sawed through, two slabs (A and B) are inserted. Then the sections of the separate boxes are pulled apart to show Nancy cut into two pieces.

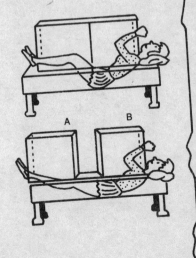

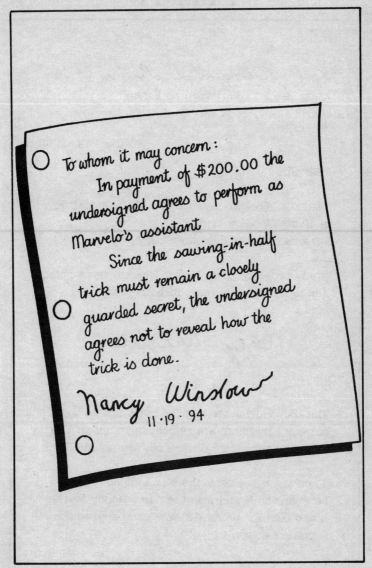

EXHIBIT C

Armand L. Poitiers
Handwriting Expert
New Brabant.

January 14, 1995

Dear Sirs:

I submit herewith my analysis of the signature
of Nancy Winslow written on a secrecy
agreement dated November 19, 1994.

In my presence, Miss Nancy Winslow has written
her signature. It is reproduced herein:

Nancy Winslow

The above signature and the signature on the
secrecy agreement are remarkably similar. The
following significant differences are noted:

1) on the agreement, there is a slight break
between the N and A in the name Nancy and the
L and O in the name Winslow, compared to the
signature above;

2) the upward extension of the W in the last
letter of the name Winslow is slightly irregular
on the agreement.

When a genuine signature is written, it usually
glides over the paper. However, a forger will
often pause and lift the pen away from the paper
as he writes. This could account for the above
differences.

Unfortunately, there is too little handwriting to
render an expert opinion. The signatures are
remarkably similar, but the possibility exists that
the secrecy agreement was not signed by Nancy
Winslow.

Respectfully yours,

Armand Poitier

VERDICT

THE SECRECY CONTRACT WAS A FORGERY.

Troy Lightfoot told the court that he tore out a blank sheet of paper from his notepad and gave it to Marvelo. But in EXHIBIT B, the sheet from the loose-leaf notepad has its holes unbroken. It could not have been torn out without ripping the holes.

Marvelo wrote the secrecy contract later on another sheet of paper that he removed carefully from the stage manager's notepad. Then he forged Nancy Winslow's signature at the bottom.

THE CASE OF THE
FLOATING LOGS

LADIES AND GENTLEMEN OF THE JURY:

If a person finds something that no one else claims, the finder can keep it. But he must give it back if the rightful owner turns up.

Keep this point of law in mind as you hear the case presented to you today.

Oswald Winters, the plaintiff, has a 30-acre farm along the Borden River. Winters accuses Sam Spooner, the defendant, of stealing logs from his farm and floating them down the river to his own land. But the defendant says Winters is mistaken and insists the logs are his.

Oswald Winters' farm is in Bordentown, located next to Spooner's farm. Both Winters and Spooner are wheat farmers, but Winters also harvests trees and sells them to a lumber mill downstream.

Oswald Winters testified as follows:

"It was on the night of August 12 that my logs disappeared. My helper and I had been working hard all day, cutting down trees. We moved the logs to the river bank next to my barn. Then we made them into a pile and tied them all together with thick ropes.

"I last remember seeing the pile of logs at about nine o'clock at night. But the next morning they were gone. The ropes had snapped."

EXHIBIT A shows the ropes that Winters used to tie his logs. Notice that both are broken.

"At first I thought that the ropes had snapped during the night and the logs rolled into the river. They must have floated downstream."

But Oswald Winters could not understand how the ropes had broken. He became suspicious. He wondered whether someone had entered his farm during the night and cut them on purpose.

The morning Winters discovered that the logs were missing, he searched the area. He was surprised to discover a set of footprints on a dirt path by the river bank. They came from the direction of Spooner's farm. Another set of footprints led back towards Spooner's farm.

EXHIBIT B shows the tracks that Winters found.

Oswald Winters continued his testimony:

"Do you see that tree lying across the path? My worker and I had cut it down the day before, and I hadn't noticed any footprints on the path then.

"The footprints must have been made between the time I cut down the tree and the time I found my logs missing the next morning.

"They must have been made by the person who entered my farm during the night and sliced the ropes.

"Then I remembered that my worker, Ezra Train, had seen Spooner near my farm on the evening that my logs rolled into the river.

"I immediately drove over to Sam Spooner's farmhouse. I couldn't believe what I saw. There, next to the Borden River on Spooner's land, was a pile of logs. I was sure it was mine! It proved Spooner went to my farm that night. He was the one who cut the ropes."

Winters' farm worker was called to the stand.

"Ezra Train is my name. I have been with Mr Winters for some fifteen years now. Mr Winters is a hardworking farmer. He's always been a very good boss."

Under questioning, Train testified as follows:

Q: What time did you see Sam Spooner on the evening that the ropes broke?

A: It was very dark. I think it must have been around ten o'clock at night. I was out walking my dog.

Q: And when did you last see Mr Winters' logs tied up by his barn?

A: I'd say it was about an hour or so before I met Spooner. The barn has a spotlight on top, so the logs were easy to see.

Q: Are you certain that the person you saw on the land was Spooner? Could you have been mistaken in the dark?

A: It was definitely Spooner. I shone my flashlight on him. He was wearing a T-shirt and shorts.

Q: Did Mr Spooner have a flashlight, too?

A: No. He wasn't carrying anything. He was walking in the pitch dark.

Q: Did Mr Spooner say where he was going?

A: He told me that he was strolling around his farm to get some fresh air. He said he must have wandered on to Mr Winters' farm by mistake.

Oswald Winters believes that when Ezra met

his neighbour, Spooner was really heading for the path to Winters' farmhouse. Under the light of the barn, Spooner cut the ropes, sending the logs into the Borden River towards his own farm.

Next, Sam Spooner, the defendant, was called to the stand. He testified as follows:

"The logs on my land don't belong to Oswald Winters. And Winters can't prove otherwise. I found the logs a week before Winters lost his. They were floating down the Borden River. They came from another farm upstream that never claimed them."

The defence entered into evidence EXHIBIT C. It is a map showing farms along the Borden River. Several of them are tree farms. Winters' and Spooner's properties are clearly marked. The map also shows the dirt path between the two farms.

Under questioning, Sam Spooner responded as follows:

Q: Mr Winters says that the footprints leading from your farm to his were made the night the ropes were cut. Are they yours?

A: Yes, those are my footprints. But they were made by me in the afternoon, not at night. I had walked over to Winters' house around four o'clock to borrow some tools. Winters wasn't there so I left.

Q: But Ezra Train said he saw you walking on Winters' farm that evening. Where were you going?

A: I was out for a walk. But I didn't go anywhere near Winters' barn that night.

Spooner continued, "I found the logs floating down the river a week before." They did not come from Winters' farm, but from a farm upstream.

"It is a case of finders keepers. Since none of the other farmers claimed them, they are rightfully mine."

LADIES AND GENTLEMEN OF THE JURY:

You have just heard the Case of the Floating Logs. You must decide the merits of Oswald Winters' claim.

Did Sam Spooner cut loose Oswald Winters' logs the night they were tied by the river bank? Or were the logs on Spooner's farm unclaimed by someone else?

EXHIBIT A

EXHIBIT B

EXHIBIT C

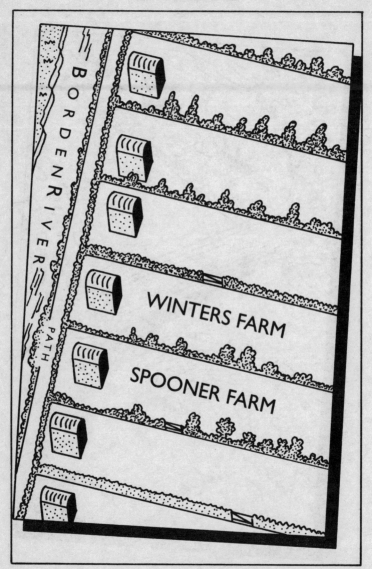

VERDICT

SOMEONE ELSE CUT THE ROPES.

Winters said that the ropes were cut during the night and that Spooner's fresh footprints on the dirt path prove he did it.

In EXHIBIT B, Spooner's prints head in the direction of the fallen tree blocking the path, and then turn towards the grass to walk around it.

This could only happen if it were daylight, when Spooner could have seen the fallen tree. If it were at night, the footprints would have been in a straight line and Spooner would have stumbled over the tree in the dark.

THE CASE OF THE
SLOPPY EATER

LADIES AND GENTLEMEN OF THE JURY:

If a person damages someone's property, he or she must pay for the repair. But there must be proof that the accused person really did the damage.

Consider the necessity for proof as you review the case presented here today.

Edgar "Smiley" Hooper, the owner of Smiley's Coffee Shop, accuses Norma Quirk of carving a long deep scratch into a wooden table top at his restaurant. Norma Quirk, the defendant, claims she is innocent. She says the damage was caused by someone else.

Smiley Hooper testified as follows:

"Miss Quirk came into my coffee shop at about 12.30, during our busy lunch time. She looked rather weird. She wore earrings as big as bracelets and a long dark skirt trailing to the floor.

"Miss Quirk sat down at a table in the rear of my shop. I handed her a menu and later came back to take her order. But she said she couldn't decide what to eat."

As soon as she was seated, Miss Quirk put her handbag on the table. Then she took out a long pointed metal nail file and started to file her nails.

Smiley continued his testimony:

"Ugh! It was disgusting to see someone filing their nails at my lunch table. But I didn't say anything.

"I came back to the table three times before the woman finally gave me her order. She asked for a Giant Blimp sandwich.

"Between filing her nails and eating her Blimp, she must have been at the table for more than half an hour. Finally, Miss Quirk asked for the bill."

The woman paid her bill and then left the restaurant. When Smiley picked up the plate to clean the table, he was shocked to see that a deep scratch had been cut in the table top. He was certain the woman with the nail file had done it.

This damaged wooden table top is presented as EXHIBIT A.

Smiley ran out of the door after Norma

Quirk. In the distance, he spotted a woman wearing a long dark skirt. He finally caught up with Miss Quirk and directed her back to his restaurant.

Smiley continued his testimony:

Q: Mr Smiley, what did the defendant say when you accused her of scratching your table?

A: I showed her the damage. She seemed very surprised and a little frightened and told me I had made a mistake. She insisted another customer must have done it.

Q: Could you have mistaken the table that Miss Quirk was sitting at? Is it possible it was someone else's plate you picked up?

A: Well, we were very busy. But I'm sure she was the one who did it. She must have used that pointed metal nail file of hers.

Then Smiley noticed pieces of onion and slices of hot pepper on the scratched table. There were also some on the chair.

Now Smiley was certain this was the table where Miss Quirk had sat. The onions and hot peppers had come from her Giant Blimp.

A photo of the crumbs that Smiley found is entered as EXHIBIT B.

Smiley says it will cost $50 to revarnish the table top. He wants the court to make Miss Quirk pay for it.

Norma Quirk was then called to the stand. "Smiley has made a terrible mistake," she said. "I did not carve that scratch in his table. I didn't even sit there. I ate at the table next to it."

Under questioning, Miss Quirk answered as follows:

Q: Do you admit you were filing your nails at the table?

A: Of course I do. Smiley was so slow in bringing me my Blimp that I decided to keep myself busy.

Q: Was your nail file strong enough to make the scratch mark?

A: I suppose so. But just because I had a nail file doesn't mean that I did it. Some people in the shop were eating with knives and forks. The scratch could have been made with one of their knives.

Q: Is it possible that you scratched the table accidentally, and didn't realize it?

A: No. Definitely not! As I told you, I wasn't sitting at the table that had the deep scratch.

Q: What about the onions and hot pepper slices that were found on the table and chair? Do you admit you were eating a Giant Blimp?

A: Yes, I ordered a Blimp. But I wasn't the only one in the shop who ate one. Besides, the menu at Smiley's has other sandwiches with onions and hot peppers. Whoever sat at that table could have ordered any one of them.

EXHIBIT C is the menu of Smiley's Coffee Shop. Note that three different sandwiches have onions and hot peppers.

Miss Quirk says Smiley has made a terrible mistake. He has mixed her up with someone else. Smiley was so busy that he had forgotten at which table she was sitting.

Miss Quirk insists she is innocent. Simply because she was filing her nails at the table does not prove that she made the scratch on it.

LADIES AND GENTLEMEN OF THE JURY:

You have just heard the Case of the Sloppy Eater. You must decide the merits of Smiley Hooper's claim. Be sure to examine carefully the evidence in EXHIBITS A, B and C.

Did Norma Quirk make the deep scratch in the coffee shop table, or was it someone else?

EXHIBIT A

EXHIBIT C

SMILEY'S COFFEE SHOP

MENU

BLIMPS

Mini-Blimp (4 inches) ham, cheese, peppers, onions, ... $2.50

Giant-Blimp (8 inches) ham, cheese, peppers, onions, ... $3.00

Monster-Blimp (12 inches) ham, cheese, peppers, onions, salami, bacon $5.00

SANDWICHES

Cheese & Tomato $2.50

Egg & Cress $1.75

Pizza Sandwich $2.25

Tuna $2.50

Ham & Cheese $2.75

PASTA AND BAKED DISHES

Ravioli $4.25

Tagliatelli $4.25

Stuffed Shells $4.75

Lasagna $4.75

Served with Salad, Bread & Butter

SERVICE WITH A SMILE

VERDICT

THE DEEP SCRATCH WAS MADE BY SOMEONE ELSE.

EXHIBIT B shows the pieces of onion and pepper on the scratched table and chair.

Smiley told the court that Norma Quirk was wearing a long dark skirt. It would have been impossible for the pieces to fall on the chair if Miss Quirk had sat there. The crumbs would have fallen on to her skirt instead. Her chair would have been perfectly clean.

Norma Quirk was innocent. She had sat at a different table.

THE CASE OF THE MISSING
HOUSEKEEPER

LADIES AND GENTLEMEN OF THE JURY:

An employment agency is a company that finds jobs for people. Before they are employed, the agency is expected to check these people out very carefully to be certain they are qualified and trustworthy.

Judith Snipes, the plaintiff, claims that a housekeeper she hired from Apex Employment Agency stole money from her bedroom drawer. Snipes is suing Apex Employment Agency, the defendant, to recover it. But the agency says there is no proof that its worker committed a crime.

Judith Snipes testified as follows:

"For as long as I can remember, my housekeeper, Mabel, worked for our family. When she retired, I didn't know where to look to replace her.

"A friend told me that Apex Employment Agency might be able to help. I met Walter Ford, the manager, and described the kind of person I wanted.

"The agency sent me several people. I finally selected Cleo Najak. She had recently moved to our country from Tangolia, but could speak English quite well. The agency said that Cleo was a hard worker and a very good cook. I really like Tangolian food, so she seemed perfect."

Cleo's first week on the job went very well. She was a quiet person, but kept the house tidy and made delicious Tangolian meals.

Then Mrs Snipes explained what happened on the afternoon of June 6:

"I was outside on my patio, asking Cleo to clean the patio furniture. Then I remembered it was time for my medicine. I asked Cleo to go to my bedroom and get it.

"When she didn't return, I went inside to find out why. As I entered the bedroom, I saw Cleo lying flat on the floor in a daze.

"She explained that as she was fetching my medicine, a masked man stepped out from behind the bedroom door. He hit her on the face with the back of his hand and fled. She fell down and blacked out."

Mrs Snipes saw that the bottom bureau drawer had been pulled out. She kept her money for the week hidden in an old purse inside the drawer. The purse was open and the money had gone.

Mrs Snipes immediately called the police. Two officers arrived and rushed upstairs. One helped Cleo while the other examined the bedroom. EXHIBIT A, taken from the police files, shows the open bureau drawer.

Mrs Snipes applied a towel soaked in cold water to Cleo's bruise and told her not to try to sit up. She was still a bit dazed.

EXHIBIT B is a photograph of the housekeeper lying on the bedroom floor. She had closed her eyes as the policemen searched for clues.

Judith Snipes continued her testimony:

"Ten days after the robbery, Cleo just walked out on me. She vanished without a trace. I couldn't understand it.

"She had taken all her belongings. But in a corner of her wardrobe I found a shopping bag she had left behind, and I looked through it. A worn out jacket was in the bag. Inside a pocket I found two credit cards with the name Sylvia Cole printed on them.

"Suddenly I realized that Cleo Najak must

have used a different name, Sylvia Cole, on her days off. Fake credit cards are used by a professional thief to buy things without paying the bill. That proves Cleo Najak was dishonest. She posed as a housekeeper so that she could find out where I kept my money."

Judith Snipes is suing Apex Employment Agency for referring a dishonest person to her. They had not checked the housekeeper out carefully. She wants the agency to pay back the money Cleo stole.

Walter Ford, manager of Apex Employment Agency, took the stand. He stated that Judith Snipes had wrongly accused his company. Ford testified as follows:

"Just because Cleo Najak left strange credit cards behind does not mean that she was a thief. Perhaps she had found them and planned to trace the owner.

"It is not uncommon for our workers to pack up and leave without notice. It usually happens when they are unhappy with the person they work for."

Mr Ford stated that shortly before Cleo left, she had telephoned his office and complained about the way she was being treated. Mrs Snipes ordered her around and yelled at her when she didn't like her work. The housekeeper told Ford she was thinking of leaving.

Under questioning, Ford described how his agency checks workers before referring them for hire:

Q: Please explain your screening procedure.

A: I am proud to say that we are very careful about the workers we choose. First we evaluate the person's appearance, to see that he or she is well groomed and has a pleasing personality. Then we go on to the next step.

Q: And what is that?

A: We contact the person they worked for in their last job. In Cleo's case, she gave us a letter of recommendation from the woman she worked for in Tangolia.

Q: What did the letter say?

A: It was from a Mrs Kaynam. She wrote that Cleo had been her housekeeper for six years. Mrs Kaynam was very satisfied and was sorry to see her go, but Cleo wanted to move to another country.

Q: Could the letter have been a fake? Could Cleo have written it herself?

A: Well, I suppose so. We usually follow up references with a phonecall, but since Mrs

Kaynam was from a foreign country, we were not able to contact her.

Q: Do you check anything else?

A: Well, we did ask Cleo for her passport. A passport will not be issued if a person has a criminal background.

The defendent entered in evidence EXHIBIT C, a photocopy of the housekeeper's passport. Her name is listed as Cleo Najak.

Ford stated his agency's position:

"Cleo's departure after the robbery was just a coincidence. There is no proof that she committed the crime. We ask the court to dismiss the law suit against our agency because we believe there is no reasonable basis for the complaint."

LADIES AND GENTLEMEN OF THE JURY:

You have just heard the Case of the Missing Housekeeper. You must decide the merits of Judith Snipes' claim. Be sure to examine carefully the evidence in EXHIBITS A, B and C.

Did the housekeeper steal Mrs Snipes' money? Or was it taken by a masked robber?

EXHIBIT A

EXHIBIT B

EXHIBIT C

NOM – NAME

CLEO NAJAK

SEXE – SEX   LIEU DE NAISSANCE – BIRTHPLACE

F   **NIBO, TANGOLIA**

EPOUSE/EPOUX – WIFE/HUSBAND   EXPIRE LE – EXPIRES ON

X X X   **February 3 1998**

DATE DE NAISSANCE – BIRTH DATE   DATE DE DELIVRANCE – ISSUE DATE

October 12, 1971   **February 4 1993**

SIGNATURE DU TITULARIE
SIGNATURE OF BEARER   *Cleo Najak*

VERDICT

THE HOUSEKEEPER STOLE THE MONEY.

In EXHIBIT B, the housekeeper is shown still lying on the floor when the police arrived. She claimed she was carrying Mrs Snipes' medicine when she was knocked down by a masked robber.

But the medicine bottle is standing upright next to her. If Cleo had really fainted, the medicine bottle would have landed on its side when she fell. It would have been impossible for it to remain upright.

The housekeeper had faked the robbery, but she had mistakenly placed the upright bottle next to her when she lay down.

THE CASE OF THE
STOLEN ANTIQUE

LADIES AND GENTLEMEN OF THE JURY:

Whenever a theft occurs, the following question should be considered: Did the victim of the robbery fake the crime in order to collect the insurance money?

Today, you must decide whether the plaintiff, Herman Stone, was indeed the victim of a theft. Empire Insurance Company, the defendant, believes that the crime was faked. It refuses to pay his insurance claim.

Mr Stone has given the following testimony:

"My friends call me 'Herman the repair man'. I own an electrical repair shop on a small street on the north side of town. I repair all kinds of appliances such as TV sets, stereos and microwave ovens. You break it – I'll fix it.

"On February 2, I was at my workbench at the back of the shop, rewiring an antique

Tiffany lamp. That's when this man walked in. I remember it very clearly. It was about 2.15 in the afternoon.

"I had never seen the man before. He was wearing an overcoat and gloves, and a hat was pulled down over his forehead. The man showed me a Walkman and said it needed new earphones.

"I searched through my stock but none of the earphones fitted the Walkman. I thought I might have a set in the basement. That's where I keep my spare parts."

Mr Stone asked the customer to wait while he went downstairs. As he was looking through his shelves, Stone heard the sound of footsteps from the customer upstairs. The man was walking around his shop.

The shop owner grew uneasy. Then he heard a noise that sounded as though tools had fallen on the floor. Stone quickly ran up the steps.

He was shocked by what he saw. The customer had gone and his cash register was open and completely empty.

Stone immediately went to check the back room for the Tiffany lamp. It had gone. Tools and parts were scattered on the floor. The thief had knocked them off the workbench when he picked up the heavy lamp.

Stone noticed that the back door was slightly

open. He always kept it locked.

The police arrived in minutes. When they searched the shop, they discovered important evidence that the thief had left behind. He had dropped his Walkman as he carried the lamp out of the back door.

EXHIBIT A is a photograph that was taken when the police arrived. It shows the rear of Stone's shop. The radio is lying on the floor.

The Walkman was sent to the police laboratory and examined for fingerprints. But the stranger had worn gloves. The only fingerprints identified were those of Mr Stone, who had handled the Walkman.

Stone explained that the crime was easily committed. First the thief took the money from the cash register. Then he went through the small gate that separated the front of the store from the back. He saw the Tiffany lamp, picked it up, and fled out of the back door.

EXHIBIT B shows the front of the repair shop. It is separated from the back by a wall. It was a simple matter for the thief to sneak to the back of the store.

Stone claims that the Tiffany lamp was a very valuable antique. He had purchased it at an auction for a customer whose house he was rewiring.

He entered as evidence EXHIBIT C, a photograph of the Tiffany lamp. It is hand crafted with richly coloured glass and is more than seventy years old.

Stone is suing Empire Insurance Company because it is unwilling to pay for his loss. He says the Tiffany lamp had cost him $4,000, and the cash register contained approximately $200.

But Empire Insurance Company believes that there was no theft and refuses to pay Stone's claim.

Lester Fenwick, an insurance investigator for the company, was called to testify. Under questioning, he answered as follows:

Q: Would you explain to the court why your company refuses to pay the plaintiff's insurance claim?

A: Based on my investigation, I believe the theft took place under very suspicious circumstances.

Q: Please tell the court exactly what you mean.

A: Well, first of all, how could a thief have known that there was a valuable antique lamp in the back of the shop? Electrical repair shops do not usually have expensive antiques. And a wall blocked the view into the back room.

Q: Do you have any other reasons for your suspicions?

A: Yes. I find it surprising that there were no fingerprints on the Walkman, except for those of Mr Stone. Even if the customer was wearing gloves, an old set of his fingerprints should have been on the radio, but none were found.

Lester Fenwick believes that Stone faked the robbery so that he could collect the insurance money. Then he could secretly sell the Tiffany lamp to someone else.

"On further investigation, I found that Stone was in serious financial trouble," explained Mr Fenwick. "His business had dropped off when another repair shop opened up nearby in a large shopping centre. It was in a more convenient position than Stone's shop.

"Then I checked to see if Mr Stone had been paying his bills on time. I discovered that his rent had not been paid for more than three months, and the telephone company had threatened to cut him off because his bills were unpaid.

"This proves that Mr Stone was badly in need of money. Collecting on a fake insurance claim would be an easy way to pull himself out of debt.

"It all adds up to one thing. There never was a theft. Mr Stone faked the whole thing to collect from Empire Insurance Company."

LADIES AND GENTLEMEN OF THE JURY:

You have just heard the Case of the Stolen Antique. You must decide the merits of Herman Stone's claim. Be sure to examine carefully the evidence in EXHIBITS A, B and C.

Did someone steal the Tiffany lamp? Or did Stone fake the theft to collect insurance money?

EXHIBIT A

EXHIBIT B

EXHIBIT C

VERDICT

STONE FAKED THE THEFT.

In EXHIBIT A, a screwdriver can be seen lying near the partly open door. If a thief had carried the large Tiffany lamp out of the back door, the screwdriver could not be lying so close to it. The screwdriver would have been moved to the side when the door was pulled fully open.

Stone faked the crime to collect the insurance money.

THE CASE OF THE BARGAIN
BEDROOM SUITE

LADIES AND GENTLEMEN OF THE JURY:

When two shops are competing with each other for customers, and one is dishonest, the shop that loses trade as a result can sue for lost business.

Keep this in mind as you review the facts in the case presented here today.

Arthur Perkins, the plaintiff, is the owner of Perkins' Furniture Shop. He accuses his competitor, Simon Quade, of making up a phony newspaper ad for Perkins' store. Perkins' customers became so angry that they switched to Quade's shop.

Mr Perkins explained to the court why he is suing Simon Quade:

"When I opened my shop for business on the morning of 26th March, I couldn't believe what I saw. There was a long line of people waiting outside. I unlocked the door and they pushed their way in.

"The first customer said he wanted to buy the bedroom suite that I advertised in the previous day's newspaper for the sale price of $80. I knew I had never put out an ad like that, but he pulled it out of his pocket and showed me. There it was, an ad with my shop's name on it, promoting an $80 bedroom suite. I told him it was a mistake."

This advertisement is shown in EXHIBIT A.

When the other customers overheard Perkins, they became angry. Soon the shop was in an uproar. When Perkins tried to calm the crowd, everyone started to leave. People shouted that they would never buy anything from his shop again.

Mr Perkins continued his testimony:

Q: Mr Perkins, is it possible that you actually placed the ad but just made an honest mistake about the price?

A: Absolutely not! I had never seen the advertisement before. Why, a bedroom suite like that sells for at least $320!

Q: Then how do you think the ad with your shop's name on it got into the newspaper?

A: How do I think it got in? I *know* how it got

in. Simon Quade put it in the newspaper and pretended it was from my shop.

Q: Why would Mr Quade make up the ad with your shop's name on it?

A: Well, until last year we were friendly competitors. Then I started to sell the same furniture for less than he did. When Quade had a desk in his store for $150, I would sell it for $110. When he had a table priced at $120, I would offer the same one for $30 less.

Soon people stopped buying from Simon Quade and shopped at Perkins' store instead.

The plaintiff continued his testimony:

"When Quade began losing business, he telephoned and told me I should stop cutting my prices. He said that if I didn't, he would find a way to get even. He actually threatened me!"

The plantiff believes that Quade was the one who put the fake ad in the newspaper because he knew customers would be angry with Perkins' Furniture Shop. Then they would go to Quade's shop instead.

Simon Quade, the defendant, then took the stand. He claimed to know nothing about Perkins' bedroom suite advert.

Mr Quade accuses Perkins of placing the advertisement in the newspaper himself. He stated that Perkins was always advertising low prices, but this time his price was too low. He just made a mistake.

Simon Quade asks that the charges against him be dismissed.

Dennis Zipp, from the *Post Tribune* newspaper, was called as the next witness. He testified as follows:

"Dennis Zipp is my name. I am in charge of all advertising for the *Post Tribune*. I see a lot of lawyers here in court. Do any of you want to advertise in our newspaper? Our rates are a real bargain!

"The reason I have been asked to testify is because some of the advertisements we print are sent to us in unfinished form. The advertiser gives us the wording and we design the ad for him. That is the way we receive advertisements for Perkins' Furniture Store."

EXHIBIT B is a letter Zipp received from Perkins' Furniture Store that the plaintiff claims is a fake. It contains the wording that his newspaper made into an advertisement.

Mr Zipp was questioned further:

Q: When did you receive the ad?

A: It arrived by post earlier in the week.

Q: Did it seem strange to you that the price was so low?

A: I never really noticed. We receive so many ads. I had it set in type just like the letter said.

Q: Does your newspaper check out the final ad with the advertiser, before it is printed in your newspaper?

A: We do usually – it depends. Mr Perkins told us we did not have to check his ads with him if they arrived very late. He often sent us ads at the last minute.

Lawyers for the plaintiff offered further proof that Quade was the person who falsely placed Perkins' low-priced ad in the newspaper. They said that Quade ran an advertisement on the same day the fake ad appeared. It warned customers to beware of advertisements promoting very low prices because it was a dishonest trick to lure them into a shop.

Mr Zipp submitted as evidence the advertisement he received from Quade. It is entered as EXHIBIT C.

The ad warns customers about "bait-and-switch" schemes that other furniture shops might use. When a customer tries to buy the low-priced furniture, the shop claims that it is all sold out. Then a clever salesman tries to switch the customer to higher priced furniture.

Mr Perkins' lawyer claims there is something very suspicious about the envelopes in EXHIBIT B and EXHIBIT C. The postmarks on the letter containing Perkins' ad and the one containing Quade's ad both have the same date. That means that the letters were posted to the newspaper *on the same day.*

He believes this is more than just a coincidence. He accuses Simon Quade of posting *both* letters. He said that Quade typed the letter on headed stationery from Perkins' Furniture Shop so it could not be traced to him.

Arthur Perkins is suing Simon Quade for the business he lost when customers stopped coming to his shop. The identical postmarks on both letters prove that the two advertisements were sent to the *Post Tribune* by Simon Quade.

LADIES AND GENTLEMEN OF THE JURY:

You have just heard the Case of the Bargain Bedroom Suite. You must decide the merits of Arthur Perkins' claim.

Be sure to examine carefully the evidence in EXHIBITS A, B and C.

Did Simon Quade send in a fake advertisement for Perkins' Furniture Shop? Or did Mr Perkins place the advertisement himself and make a mistake about the price?

SALE· OF THE YEAR
OUR LOWEST PRICES EVER!!!

6-piece Contemporary Natural Oak Bedroom Suite.
Includes headboard, dressing table, mirror,
2 night stands and chest of drawers.

ONLY $80

PERKIN'S FURNITURE STORE
28 DUNCAN AVENUE

PERKINS' FURNITURE STORE

June 6, 1995

Dear Sirs

Please set the ad below in type and run it in your Sunday newspaper of 12th June. Use the same picture of the bedroom set that was in my 5th June advertisement in your newspaper:

SALE OF THE YEAR!!

OUR LOWEST PRICE EVER!!!!

6 piece Contemporary Natural Oak Bedroom Suite. Includes headboard, dresser, mirror, 2 night stands and chest.

only $80 (use large print for the price)

Yours sincerely,

Arthur Perkins

ARTHUR PERKINS

Advertising Department

Post Tribune Newspaper

64 Squire St.

Peadmont

EXHIBIT C

QUADE'S FURNITURE STORE

6·6·95

Dear Sirs.

Please run the ad below in your Sunday edition.

Thank you

Very truly Yours

Simon Quade.

DON'T BE CHEATED BY PHONY FURNITURE ADS

QUADE'S PRICES ARE THE LOWEST!

Other shops may advertise furniture at ridiculously low prices. But when you go to buy

Advertising Department
Post Tribune Newspaper
64 Square Street
Piedmont, OHIO

EXHIBIT C

it, they claim they are all sold out. Then they
try to interest you in buying other furniture
at a much higher price!

Beware of tricky ''bait-and-switch'' ads.
Buy only from a shop you can trust.
AND QUADE'S PRICES ARE THE LOWEST!

A public service message from
Quade's Furniture Shop

VERDICT

QUADE SENT THE FAKE AD TO
THE NEWSPAPER.

The stamp on the envelope in EXHIBIT B
that is supposedly from Perkins' Furniture
Shop is torn irregularly. It has two
indentations.

The shape of the indentations matches the
pieces attached to the stamp in EXHIBIT C,
from the letter sent by Quade's Furniture
Shop. The pieces fit together exactly.
This proves that the stamps were next to
each other on the same stamp sheet, before
they were torn off and stuck on the two
envelopes. Since they came from the same
sheet, the letters were sent by the same person.
Quade had sent both advertisements.

THE CASE OF THE
TORN SHIRT

LADIES AND GENTLEMEN OF THE JURY:

The act of robbery is a criminal offence. If the property stolen is very valuable, the thief can be sent to prison for a long time.

Since we are in criminal court today, the State is the accuser. The State charges Perry Scruggs, the defendant, with stealing a pearl necklace. Scruggs claims he is innocent and that someone else committed the crime.

The robbery occurred at four o'clock on the afternoon of 7th July, when Jennifer Horner was walking home from her friend's birthday party.

Jennifer Horner testified as follows:

"I had taken a short cut through Mayberry Park. I was wearing my new dress and a long strand of pearls. As I walked along a path, I heard footsteps behind me. I sensed I was being followed.

"I was about to turn around when I received a heavy blow on the back of my head. I fell to the ground and blacked out."

Jennifer awoke, half-dazed. When she realized where she was, she felt her neck. The pearl necklace she had been wearing was gone.

Jennifer staggered towards the park entrance and saw a policeman in the distance. She waved frantically and Officer Archy Stevens ran over to her. Jennifer cried out that her necklace had been stolen.

Officer Stevens was called to the witness stand to explain why he had arrested the defendant.

"My name is Archy Stevens. I have been a proud member of the Mayberry police force for eight years. I have two commendations for bravery.

"After I calmed Miss Horner down, I examined the ground where she fell. A dirty metal pole was lying nearby. It must have been used to hit her over the head. I also noticed fresh footprints next to the pole."

A close-up photograph of the footprints and pole is shown in EXHIBIT A. Note the unusual footprint design.

The policeman continued his testimony:

"I also found a torn rag lying on the grass near the robbery. It was streaked with dirt marks. The robber must have used it to wipe his fingerprints off the pole."

The policeman realized that the torn rag came from a grey shirt. In the corner of the rag, above the pocket, he found part of a name tape showing the first two letters, "PE".

Officer Stevens noticed a large storage shed at one end of the park. He told Jennifer to rest and then rushed over to it.

Two workers were inside, painting park benches. They stopped and looked up when the officer entered.

As Officer Stevens questioned the men, he saw that they both wore park shirts that were the same colour as the torn rag. The men identified themselves as Frank Hudson and Perry Scruggs.

The first name of each worker was sewn above his shirt pocket. The letters on Perry Scruggs' shirt looked exactly like the first two letters on the torn rag.

EXHIBIT B is a photo taken by Officer Stevens inside the shed. A picture of the torn rag is clipped to it. The letters of Scruggs' shirt match the torn rag.

The policeman then asked Scruggs to lift up

his shoe. The pattern on the sole was similar to the footprints near the robbery.

Officer Stevens determined that Scruggs' shoes were the same size as those at the crime scene, and the pattern matched exactly. On this basis, he placed Scruggs under arrest.

The State called Frank Hudson as its first witness. He said that both he and Perry Scruggs were in the storage shed painting park benches for more than two hours. The necklace was stolen during this time.

Under questioning, Hudson admitted that they had not been together in the storage shed the whole time. Scruggs had left for about twenty minutes to apply a fresh coat of paint to a water fountain. Then he had returned and continued working on the benches.

The State estimates that Perry Scruggs had left the shed during the time Jennifer Horner was robbed. Scruggs had no alibi when the robbery occurred.

Perry Scruggs, the defendant, took the stand. He insists that he is innocent of the crime. He testified as follows:

Q: Did anyone see you painting the water fountain when you left the shed?

A: No. I was the only person near the fountain.

But if you're thinking I was the one who sneaked up behind the lady, then you're wrong.

Q: Does the torn rag belong to you?

A: It looks as if it came from an old shirt of mine. All park workers rip up their worn out shirts and use them for cleaning rags. We keep them in a box inside the storage shed.

Q: How do you think it got to the scene of the crime?

A: Someone must have been using a cleaning rag with my name on it. That's how!

Q: But what about your footprints? How did they get there?

A: Those footprints aren't mine. They were made by a person who wears the same shoes that I wear. He must have the same size feet. Mayberry Park has a dozen workers. We all wear the same work shoes. And some of us have the same shoe size.

Perry Scruggs told the court that another park worker must have committed the robbery. He had dropped Scruggs' torn shirt near the scene of the crime.

As proof of Scruggs' claim, the defence showed the court EXHIBIT C. It is a photograph taken at the beginning of the season, showing all the park workers.

Perry Scruggs is the first person on the left, in the front row. Notice that all the workers have park shirts and they all are wearing identical shoes.

Scruggs claims the robbery was committed by another park worker. Then he used Scruggs' torn shirt to wipe his fingerprints off the pole.

LADIES AND GENTLEMEN OF THE JURY:

You have just heard the Case of the Torn Shirt. You must decide the merits of the State's accusation. Be sure to examine carefully the evidence in EXHIBITS A, B and C.

Did Perry Scruggs steal the pearl necklace or was the robbery committed by someone else?

EXHIBIT A

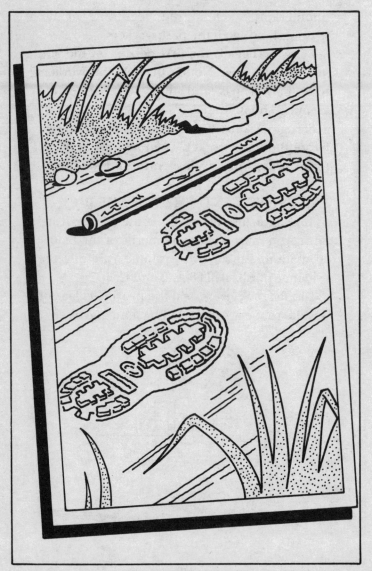

EXHIBIT C

VERDICT

SOMEONE ELSE STOLE THE NECKLACE.

The streaks on the torn shirt were made when the robber wiped his fingerprints off the pole. But in EXHIBIT B, Scruggs is shown wearing work gloves.

If Scruggs had committed the robbery, he did not need to wipe the pole clean of fingerprints. None would have been on the pole.

The robbery was committed by someone else.

101

THE CASE OF THE
REFRIGERATOR
BREAKDOWN

Ladies and Gentlemen of the Jury:

When a shop sells an appliance that breaks down, the person who bought it can have his money refunded. But if the buyer is warned at the time of purchase that the appliance is not guaranteed to have a long life, that is a very different matter.

Peter Frapp purchased a used refrigerator from Dayton City Domestic Appliances shop. It broke down after three weeks. Frapp is suing the shop to return his money. But Jeffrey Hawkins, the shop owner, claims he sold the fridge to Frapp without a guarantee and refuses to give a refund.

Peter Frapp, the plaintiff, had moved to Dayton to find work. The factory in his home town had closed. When he arrived, Frapp rented a one-room apartment on the east side of town.

Frapp wasn't very well off. He realized that by eating his meals in his room, he could stretch his savings until he found a new job. But he needed to buy a refrigerator.

While Frapp was shopping in Hamilton Street, he passed Dayton City Domestic Appliances. A large sign in the window announced a sale.

Frapp testified as follows:

"When I saw the sign, I thought I was in luck. I went inside the shop and there was Mr Hawkins behind the counter.

"Mr Hawkins showed me his cheapest fridge but I was very disappointed. It was more than I could afford. I told Mr Hawkins that I had budgeted $40. He smiled and said he had just what I wanted."

Hawkins told Frapp that he would sell him a used fridge for exactly $40. He had repaired it for a customer, but the owner had bought a new one instead.

Peter Frapp continued his testimony:

Q: Were you suspicious that something might be wrong when Mr Hawkins asked such a low price for the refrigerator?

A: Well, I really thought I was lucky to find one I could afford. Mr Hawkins told me it was only three years old, so I thought it had to be okay.

Q: Did Hawkins claim that the refrigerator was in good working order?

A: He certainly did. That's why I decided to buy it. He said that if I was not satisfied, I could return it within thirty days and get my money back.

The following day, the fridge was delivered to Frapp's home. He immediately went shopping and stocked it with food, but three weeks later the fridge stopped working. All the food was ruined.

EXHIBIT A is a photograph of Peter Frapp standing next to the broken fridge. Everything had melted or gone bad.

Frapp went back to Dayton City Domestic Appliances and demanded his money back, but Mr Hawkins refused. The owner told him that he had purchased the appliance at his own risk.

Peter Frapp was very upset. Then he had an idea. He wrote to the fridge manufacturer to find out how old the appliance really was.

The manufacturer's reply is shown in EXHIBIT B. It states that the fridge was twelve years old.

Peter Frapp was shocked when he received

the letter. Hawkins had deceived him. He is suing Jeffrey Hawkins, claiming the shop owner lied about the fridge. He is asking the court to order Hawkins to refund his $40 and the cost of the spoiled food.

Jeffrey Hawkins took the stand and testified as follows:

"I clearly remember the day Peter Frapp came into my shop. How could I forget? He was shabbily dressed and had an evil-looking scar on his face. His trousers were patched. I felt sorry for him.

"When Frapp told me how much he could afford, I knew I had nothing for that price. But I thought I would do him a favour by selling him the used fridge. It worked perfectly after I'd mended it.

"I sold the fridge at my cost. When you include the repair parts and delivery, Frapp got a real bargain.

"I warned Mr Frapp that I was not responsible if the fridge stopped working. At the price he paid, he had to buy it 'as seen'.

"And I certainly never told Frapp it was three years old. I said that I couldn't guarantee how long it would work."

Jeffrey Hawkins claimed that a witness overheard his conversation warning Frapp about the fridge. His stock clerk, Charles Crow, was working in the back room while Frapp was in the shop.

EXHIBIT C is a photograph of the interior of Dayton City Domestic Appliances. It shows the position of the stock room door. When the door is open, it is possible to overhear a conversation at the cash register.

Charles Crow, the stock room clerk, testified as follows:

Q: Mr Hawkins claims that you overheard part of his conversation with Mr Frapp. What exactly did he say?

A: Well, I was working in the back room, when I poked my head round the door to find out what time it was. Mr Hawkins was at the cash register, handing Frapp his change. I distinctly overheard their conversation.

Q: What did you hear Mr Hawkins say?

A: He was explaining to Frapp that the fridge was a used one and he couldn't guarantee how long it would work. Frapp nodded in agreement.

Q: Were those Mr Hawkins' exact words?

A: Yes. That's exactly what he said.

Q: Are you certain it was Peter Frapp who was at the cash register? Could Mr Hawkins have been explaining the guarantee to another customer instead?

A: I'm positive it was Frapp. I'd recognize him anywhere. He needed a haircut and it was hard not to notice that scar on his face. I even remember the patches on his trousers.

Q: Did Mr Hawkins say anything else?

A: I don't know. When I saw he was with a customer, I closed the door and went back to work.

Jeffrey Hawkins states that Crow's testimony supports his claim that Mr Frapp was warned about the fridge. He asks that the charges be dismissed because Frapp knew he was buying the fridge 'as seen'.

LADIES AND GENTLEMEN OF THE JURY:

You have just heard the Case of the Refrigerator Breakdown. You must decide the merits of Peter Frapp's claim. Be sure to examine carefully the evidence in EXHIBITS A, B and C.

Was Peter Frapp warned that the fridge had no guarantee? Or was the testimony against him a lie?

EXHIBIT A

EXHIBIT B

ICE AGE
REFRIGERATION COMPANY

6 March, 1995

Dear Mr Frapp

This is to acknowledge your letter of 4th February regarding an Ice Age refrigerator with the serial number SN40662.

According to our records, this refrigerator was manufactured by our company in 1983, approximately 12 years ago.

I hope this information is of help to you.

Yours sincerely,

Betty Brattle
Customer Service Manager

EXHIBIT C

VERDICT

THE TESTIMONY WAS A LIE.

Hawkins' stock clerk, Charles Crow, said he heard the shop owner warning Frapp that the fridge could not be guaranteed. He had recognized Frapp because of the scar on his face.

EXHIBIT A shows a photograph of Peter Frapp. A large scar is on his *left* cheek. But Crow's view of Peter Frapp would have been from Frapp's *right* side while he was standing at the cash register. It would have been impossible for Crow to see Frapp's scar as he was speaking to Mr Hawkins at the counter.

THE CASE OF THE
RUNAWAY CAR

LADIES AND GENTLEMEN OF THE JURY:

A person visiting an amusement park can expect to enjoy a day of fun and thrills. But it is the park's responsibility to be sure all of its rides are safe. If someone is accidentally hurt, the park is responsible.

Mrs Rhonda Pepper, the plaintiff, is in court today and has accused High Time Park of operating a dangerous ride. Because it was unsafe, she was seriously injured. The owner of High Time states that the accident was caused by Mr Pepper's carelessness.

On 12th July, a warm Sunday afternoon, Mr and Mrs Pepper took their daughter Karen to High Time Park. High Time is known as the largest amusement park in the area. It has dozens of rides, from a monster roller coaster to a scary Whirl-A-Gig.

Carl Pepper, the plaintiff's husband, explained to the court how the accident happened:

"We were at the park for several hours and went on about eight rides in all. At around five o'clock, my wife said she was getting tired and wanted to go home. But Karen pleaded with me to take her on just one more ride."

Karen asked to go on the Bump-A-Ride. It has small electrically powered cars that move around on a wooden floor. Riders drive around and bump into each other. Then the cars bounce off one another harmlessly and zigzag in another direction.

Mr Pepper continued his testimony:

"Karen was riding with me. She was having a wonderful time, laughing and screaming whenever we bumped into another car. After about five minutes, the loud clanging noise of a bell signalled that the ride was over.

"We were the last ones to leave the car. As we were about to get out, my wife hurried across the floor to meet us.

"As she rushed towards us, an empty car headed straight for my wife. She held out her hand, but it knocked her down before it stopped. As I helped her stand up, it was obvious she was in a lot of pain.

"An ambulance rushed my wife to the hospital. The doctor who examined her found that her legs were seriously bruised below the knees and the shin bone in her left leg was broken. She was in a plaster cast for six weeks."

Mr Pepper had his camera with him at the park. A photograph of his wife's accident is entered as EXHIBIT A. Mrs Pepper is in obvious pain. You will note that one trouser leg is torn where the car bumper hit her.

Before the ambulance arrived, Mr Pepper also took a photograph of the car that he said hit his wife. This is entered as EXHIBIT B. The car is the striped one on the left. Next to it is the car in which Mr Pepper and his daughter were riding.

Rhonda Pepper is suing High Time Park for unsafe operation of its Bump-A-Ride. She wants full payment for her medical costs and for her pain and suffering caused by the accident.

The manager of High Time Park took the stand. He defends the safety of the park and claims that it is not responsible for Mrs Pepper's injuries.

"Ferris Wheeler is my name. I have been general manager of High Time Park for more than eight years. Nothing like this has ever happened to us before.

"I feel sorry for Mrs Pepper, but our business was affected too. After people read about the accident, our attendance dropped off."

Under questioning, Mr Wheeler stated that a runaway car could not have caused the accident:

Q: Do you check the safety of the Bump-A-Ride cars regularly, Mr Wheeler?

A: Of course. We do it for all our rides. Each evening, after our park closes, an attendant inspects the cars to prepare for the next day. He makes certain they all are in good working order.

Q: How can you be so sure that an empty runaway car did not hit Mrs Pepper?

A: It is mechanically impossible. When a person pushes down the foot pedal, the car goes forward. When the foot lifts up, it stops. Someone has to be inside the car to move it forward. It is as simple as that!

EXHIBIT C is a photograph of the inside of a bumper car. Notice that it only has one pedal. When the pedal is pushed down the car moves forward.

The lawyer for the plaintiff continued his questioning of Mr Wheeler:

Q: What about the bumper on the front? Is the rubber flexible enough to prevent a person from being injured?

A: I don't know. The bumper is there so that cars can bump into and bounce off each other harmlessly. It is not supposed to bounce off people.

Q: Then is it possible that, even with the rubber bumper, a car could injure a person?

A: Well, I suppose so. But I am certain that Mrs Pepper was not hit by a runaway car.

Mr Wheeler gave another explanation for the accident. He believes that the only way it could have happened was if a person was driving the car that hit Mrs Pepper. The manager contends the person could have been Mr Pepper.

"Mr Pepper has stated here in court that he was the last person to get out of the car. When his wife walked on to the floor, I think Mr Pepper's foot accidentally hit the pedal and the car shot forward.

"It was his car that ran into her. The striped car was not involved."

Mr Wheeler claims that Mrs Pepper does not want to admit that her husband caused the accident, so that High Time Park will pay for her injuries.

LADIES AND GENTLEMEN OF THE JURY:

You have just heard the Case of the Runaway Car. You must decide the merits of Rhonda Pepper's claim. Be sure to examine carefully the evidence in EXHIBITS A, B and C.

Was Mrs Pepper injured by the striped runaway bumper car? Or was she hit by the car her husband was driving?

EXHIBIT A

EXHIBIT C

VERDICT

MRS PEPPER WAS HIT BY HER HUSBAND'S CAR.

EXHIBIT A shows Mrs Pepper after the accident. Both legs are injured just below her knees, but the bumper of the striped car in EXHIBIT B is too low to have caused the injury. It would have hit her ankles.

The car next to it, in which Mr Pepper rode, has a higher bumper. It is the only one of the two cars that could have caused the accident.

NOTES

NOTES

NOTES

Get a clue...
Your favorite board game is a mystery series!

by A.E. Parker

☐ BAM46110-9	#1	Who Killed Mr. Boddy?	$3.50
☐ BAM45631-8	#2	The *Secret* Secret Passage	$2.99
☐ BAM45632-6	#3	The Case of the Invisible Cat	$2.95
☐ BAM45633-4	#4	Mystery at the Masked Ball	$2.95
☐ BAM47804-4	#5	Midnight Phone Calls	$3.25
☐ BAM47805-2	#6	Booby Trapped	$3.50
☐ BAM48735-3	#7	The Picture Perfect Crime	$3.25
☐ BAM48934-8	#8	The Clue in the Shadow	$3.50
☐ BAM48935-6	#9	Mystery in the Moonlight	$3.50
☐ BAM48936-4	#10	The Case of the Screaming Skeleton	$3.50
☐ BAM62374-5	#11	Death by Candlelight	$3.50
☐ BAM62375-3	#12	The Haunted Gargoyle	$3.50
☐ BAM62376-1	#13	The Revenge of the Mummy	$3.50
☐ BAM62377-X	#14	The Dangerous Diamond	$3.50
☐ BAM13742-5	#15	The Vanishing Vampire	$3.50
☐ BAM13743-3	#16	Danger After Dark	$3.99

Available wherever you buy books, or use this order form

Scholastic Inc., P.O. Box 7502, 2931 East McCarty Street, Jefferson City, MO 65102

Please send me the books I have checked above. I am enclosing $_____ (please add $2.00 to cover shipping and handling). Send check or money order—no cash or C.O.D.s please.

Name_____Birthdate_____

Address_____

City_____State/Zip_____

Please allow four to six weeks for delivery. Offer good in U.S. only. Sorry mail orders are not available to residents of Canada. Prices subject to change.   CL996

GET
Goosebumps®
by R.L. Stine

☐ BAB45365-3	#1	Welcome to Dead House	$3.99
☐ BAB45369-6	#5	The Curse of the Mummy's Tomb	$3.99
☐ BAB49445-7	#10	The Ghost Next Door	$3.99
☐ BAB49450-3	#15	You Can't Scare Me!	$3.99
☐ BAB47742-0	#20	The Scarecrow Walks at Midnight	$3.99
☐ BAB48355-2	#25	Attack of the Mutant	$3.99
☐ BAB48348-X	#30	It Came from Beneath the Sink	$3.99
☐ BAB48349-8	#31	The Night of the Living Dummy II	$3.99
☐ BAB48344-7	#32	The Barking Ghost	$3.99
☐ BAB48345-5	#33	The Horror at Camp Jellyjam	$3.99
☐ BAB48346-3	#34	Revenge of the Lawn Gnomes	$3.99
☐ BAB48340-4	#35	A Shocker on Shock Street	$3.99
☐ BAB56873-6	#36	The Haunted Mask II	$3.99
☐ BAB56874-4	#37	The Headless Ghost	$3.99
☐ BAB56875-2	#38	The Abominable Snowman of Pasadena	$3.99
☐ BAB56876-0	#39	How I Got My Shrunken Head	$3.99
☐ BAB56877-9	#40	Night of the Living Dummy III	$3.99
☐ BAB56878-7	#41	Bad Hare Day	$3.99
☐ BAB56879-5	#42	Egg Monsters from Mars	$3.99
☐ BAB56880-9	#43	The Beast from the East	$3.99
☐ BAB56881-7	#44	Say Cheese and Die–Again!	$3.99
☐ BAB56882-5	#45	Ghost Camp	$3.99
☐ BAB56883-3	#46	How to Kill a Monster	$3.99
☐ BAB56884-1	#47	Legend of the Lost Legend	$3.99
☐ BAB56885-X	#48	Attack of the Jack-O'-Lanterns	$3.99
☐ BAB56886-8	#49	Vampire Breath	$3.99
☐ BAB56887-6	#50	Calling All Creeps	$3.99
☐ BAB56888-4	#51	Beware, the Snowman	$3.99

Scare me, thrill me, mail me GOOSEBUMPS now!

Available wherever you buy books, or use this order form. Scholastic Inc., P.O. Box 7502,
2931 East McCarty Street, Jefferson City, MO 65102

Please send me the books I have checked above. I am enclosing $_____ (please add $2.00 to cover shipping and handling). Send check or money order — no cash or C.O.D.s please.

Name_____Age _____

Address_____

City _____State/Zip_____

Please allow four to six weeks for delivery. Offer good in the U.S. only. Sorry,
mail orders are not available to residents of Canada. Prices subject to change.